# Cha___'s Big Break

By Reese Everett

Illustrated by Sally Garland

Rourke
Educational Media
rourkeeducationalmedia.com

www.rourkeeducationalmedia.com


Edited by: Keli Sipperley
Cover layout by: Renee Brady
Interior layout by: Rhea Magaro
Cover and Interior Illustrations by: Sally Garland


**Library of Congress PCN Data**

Charlie's Big Break / Reese Everett
  (Rourke's Beginning Chapter Books)
  ISBN (hard cover)(alk. paper) 978-1-63430-376-7
  ISBN (soft cover) 978-1-63430-476-4
  ISBN  (e-Book) 978-1-63430-572-3
  Library of Congress Control Number:  2015933733


Printed in the United States of America,
North Mankato, Minnesota

*Dear Parents and Teachers:*

*Realistic fiction is ideal for readers transitioning from picture books to chapter books. In Rourke's Beginning Chapter Books, young readers will meet characters that are just like them. They will be drawn in by the familiar settings of school and home and the familiar themes of sports, friendship, feelings, and family. Young readers will relate to the characters as they experience the ups and downs of growing up. At this level, making connections with characters is key to developing reading comprehension.*

*Rourke's Beginning Chapter Books offer simple narratives organized into short chapters with some illustrations to support transitional readers. The short, simple sentences help readers build the needed stamina to conquer longer chapter books.*

*Whether young readers are reading the books independently or you are reading with them, engaging with them after they have read the book is still important. We've included several activities at the end of each book to make this both fun and educational.*

*By exposing young readers to beginning chapter books, you are setting them up to succeed in reading!*

*Enjoy,*
*Rourke Educational Media*

# Table of Contents

Great News ....................................... Page 6

Ouch ................................................ Page 11

Worst Day Ever ............................... Page 15

Bummer Buddy ............................... Page 20

Picnic Party .................................... Page 25

You Must Be Kidding ...................... Page 29

Liar, Liar ......................................... Page 33

Surprise! ......................................... Page 39

# Chapter 1
# Great News

Charlie pumped her legs, the swing going higher and higher as she chattered to her friend Leo.

"I'm going to lead the whole Blueberry Festival parade!" she said, throwing her head back and smiling. She looked up at the sky and leaned back farther.

Leo laughed. He pumped his legs faster to try to get his swing as high as Charlie's. Leo and Charlie met in preschool. They'd been best friends ever since.

Both Leo and Charlie liked to be adventurous. Their parents called them "The Tornadoes." They were always trying to outdo each other. Charlie usually won. She was just a little bit braver. Leo liked that about her. They did everything together, except when Charlie was at gymnastics, Leo was playing hockey.

"I still can't believe Coach picked me. She said it's my big break!" Charlie squealed. "Will you be there?"

"My mom said we can go as long as the baby doesn't come before Saturday," Leo said. His mother was pregnant with Leo's fourth brother. They planned to name him Joe.

"Stay in there two more days, little buddy!" Charlie laughed.

The Blueberry Festival parade was the biggest party in town every year. People came from all over to watch or be a part of it. Only the best gymnastics and dance teams got to perform in the parade. Charlie's gymnastics team would be at the very front of the parade, leading the whole thing! Charlie had never been so happy. When her coach asked if she would be the team leader in the parade, she couldn't wait to tell Leo.

"Will you throw me some beads?" Leo asked.

"Of course," Charlie said. "I'll save you the best ones!"

Leo grinned and twisted in his swing, trying to make it spin. Charlie did the same.

"Time to get back to class, everyone!" Their teacher, Miss Weaver, stood up from the picnic table and gathered the papers she'd graded during recess.

"One, two, three, jump!" Charlie yelled.

She launched herself off the swing, hit the ground, and fell over.

"OWWWWWW!" Charlie screamed, clutching her leg. Tears streamed from her eyes. Leo dragged his feet to slow his swing and rushed over to her. Miss Weaver ran over, too.

She took one look at Charlie's leg and her face turned sick-looking.

"Don't move, Charlotte Grace," Miss Weaver said. "Leo, stay with her."

Miss Weaver scrambled to her feet and rushed back to the picnic table. She grabbed her walkie-talkie and spoke quickly. Leo heard her say "Call an ambulance."

# Chapter 2
# Ouch

Charlie's parents were already at the hospital when the paramedics wheeled her in on the gurney.

They rushed over and grabbed her hands.

"Are you okay, hon?" Her mom looked terrified.

"Yes, I think so." Charlie was a little bit sleepy. The paramedics told her the medicine might make her feel that way.

"She's going to be fine, ma'am," the ambulance driver told Charlie's parents. She smiled reassuringly at them. "Looks like a fracture. She will probably need a cast."

Some nurses came and wheeled Charlie through some doors and into a room that had curtains instead of walls. Her parents followed them.

"We're going to have someone come in and x-ray that leg, Charlie," a nurse with long brown hair said sweetly. She squeezed Charlie's hand. "Hang tight, we will get you all fixed up."

Charlie smiled weakly. She felt woozy and her leg throbbed.

A man came in a few minutes later with a machine on wheels. He asked how Charlie was feeling, gave her a knuckle bump, and then positioned the machine over her leg.

"Hold still, kiddo," he said.

The machine beeped and whirred. Charlie tried not to move, but it was hard because sharp pains kept shooting through her leg. When he was finished, the man moved the machine out of the way and gave her another fist bump.

"Ya did good, little lady," he said. He turned to her mom and dad. "I'll get the radiologist to look at these as soon as possible then the doctor will be in." Her parents nodded their thanks. A nurse came in and gave Charlie some more medicine.

"The parade ..." Charlie mumbled before she fell fast asleep.

She wasn't sure how long she slept before a tall woman with long blonde hair in a white coat came in and introduced herself as Dr. Palmer. She put the x-rays up on a lighted wall next to Charlie.

"See here, wild woman?" Dr. Palmer pointed to a line across the picture of Charlie's leg bone. "That is where your leg is fractured. The good news is the break doesn't go all through the bone, only part of it."

"Will I ever be able to walk again?" Charlie's mind filled with all the things she loved to do, like cartwheels and running and jumping on the trampoline with Leo. She felt sick to her stomach.

"Yes, sweetheart," Dr. Palmer smiled and squeezed Charlie's hand. 'We're going to put a cast on you and get you all fixed up. You'll be on crutches for about six weeks, though."

Dr. Palmer blew into a plastic glove, tied the ends, and drew a face on it. The glove fingers made the balloon face look like it had a Mohawk. She handed it to Charlie then said she would be right back to get the cast started.

"I can't lead the parade Saturday on crutches," Charlie said quietly after the doctor left. The itchy tears wouldn't stay in her eyes anymore. They fell down her cheeks instead.

# Chapter 3
# Worst Day Ever

Charlie sat on the couch staring at her new purple cast while her mother spoke to the gymnastics coach on the phone. *This is the worst day ever*, she thought. She twisted her long brown hair tightly around her finger, the way she always did when she was upset. Her mom patted her arm sympathetically as she talked into the phone.

"Charlie, honey, Coach wants to talk to you," her mom said. She handed her the phone.

Coach told Charlie how sorry she was about the accident and not to worry, there is always next year's parade. She also told Charlie that Karrington would have to take her place as the team leader on Saturday.

*Karrington! Ugh,* Charlie thought, the knot in her stomach getting tighter as Coach continued talking. Karrington was always saying not-nice things to Charlie at practice. She imagined Karrington's face breaking into a giant, mean grin when she heard her bad news.

There was a knock at the door soon after she hung up. Her mom came out of the kitchen to answer it. Miss Weaver stood at the door with a bunch of balloons and a box.

"Miss Weaver, come in! How nice!" Charlie's mom said, ushering her teacher into the living room. Charlie sat up a little straighter and tried to put on a happy face.

Miss Weaver tied the balloons to a table next to the couch then leaned over to give Charlie a hug. The box was full of cards her classmates made after the ambulance took her away that morning. The biggest one was from Leo. He'd taped four pieces of construction paper together to make a huge card covered with drawings of them doing fun things together. It made her smile and it also made her sad. *No more fun*, she grumped in her head. *No more parade.*

She thought she better call Leo and tell him what happened at the hospital. She wasn't ready yet, though. She didn't want to cry on the phone like a big baby. She felt like crying right now.

Miss Weaver and her mom chatted for a while about Charlie being on crutches at school and about the bake sale coming up and some other boring stuff. Charlie didn't really listen. She was thinking of all sorts of things she wouldn't be able to do and feeling very sorry for herself.

"May I sign your cast before I go?" Miss Weaver asked as she stood up to leave.

"Um, sure," Charlie said. Miss Weaver drew a funny face with huge eyes and a toothy smile.

"You're a great artist, Miss Weaver!" Charlie said when she was done. She meant it. Miss Weaver always drew funny pictures on the board at school while she taught. She would draw little bits at a time. The students always paid close attention to the lesson as they tried to figure out what the finished drawing would be. Charlie thought it was a pretty cool trick to keep them interested.

Charlie called Leo later that night. She told him everything about the hospital and the cast and mean ol' Karrington and the parade. She could hear his brothers yelling in the background as she spoke.

"What are they screaming about?" she finally asked.

"Football game on TV. They all made bets with each other or something. My mom is the one yelling the loudest," Leo said.

"Your baby brother might not be born for a while," Charlie said. 'If I were him, I'd be scared to come out."

Leo laughed.

Talking to Leo made Charlie feel better, but all of a sudden, he said he had to go.

"What's wrong?" she asked.

"Nothing, er, um, everything is fine. I'll see you at school tomorrow. Bye!" he hung up before she could say anything else.

# Chapter 4
# Bummer Buddy

The next day at school, everyone wanted to sign Charlie's cast.

"You're a real distraction around here," Miss Weaver joked. She set out permanent markers in lots of colors and gave Charlie a chair to prop her leg up on.

Leo drew two tornadoes next to each other, then signed his name. Charlie noticed he'd been very quiet all day. The other kids were so hyped up though, she didn't have much time to think about it. Everyone wanted to know everything.

"Does it hurt?"

"Not as much right now," she said.

"What did the inside of the ambulance look like?"

"There was lots of equipment and medicine and tools and stuff, I think," she said, trying to remember the ride.

"Did they have to cut your leg open?"

Charlie shuddered at that question.

"No, thank goodness!" she said. She told them all about the hospital: the way it smelled of chemicals and chicken soup, the x-ray machine on wheels, the glove balloon her doctor made.

"How long will you have to wear your cast?" a boy named Phillip asked.

"Six weeks," she grumbled. Thinking about it made her eyes itch with tears. She hid her face with her hair so no one would see.

"Recess!" Miss Weaver said. Everyone rushed out of the classroom door as Charlie struggled to get up from her chair. She looked around to ask Leo for help, but he was gone. Miss Weaver helped her, instead. She patted Charlie on her head and looked at her with an I'm-so-sorry kind of smile.

"I'll be okay," Charlie said in her bravest voice. She blinked away the tears and hobbled out of the classroom.

******

Leo was not on the playground when she got outside. Charlie sat at the picnic table with Miss Weaver and watched the other kids play.

"Where is Leo?" Charlie asked her teacher. Miss Weaver looked up from the papers she was grading. Charlie thought she had a funny look on her face for a second but then it was just a regular teacher face again.

"He went home early, dear," she said.

When Charlie asked why, Miss Weaver said she would have to ask him herself, then looked back down at the papers. She was biting her lip like she was trying not to smile.

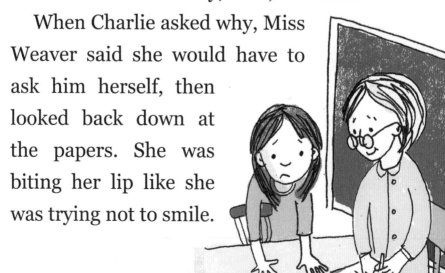

Charlie stared at her for a minute then sighed. Leo always told her everything. She didn't understand why he would leave without telling her. He hardly talked to her all morning, and now Miss Weaver was acting weird. It made her feel grumpy and sad and a little mad.

*Some best friend he is*, she thought to herself.

The rest of the day went by slower than a snail race. Charlie had a hard time concentrating because her brain kept wanting to think about why Leo wasn't there. He'd promised to tell her if his mother was having the baby. Could he have forgotten? Now that she couldn't run and play and have adventures with him, did he not want to be her best friend anymore? That thought made her stomach do a flip-flop.

By the time her mom picked her up, Charlie's head was a jumble of worry and her leg ached. A teacher helped her get into the car and put her crutches in the backseat. They stuck out of the open window a little bit.

"How was your day?" her mom asked.

"Horrible," Charlie said. She crossed her arms over her chest and slumped down in the seat. She let out a big sigh. She felt like she'd been holding her breath all day.

Her mom leaned over and kissed her cheek. "Want to talk about it?"

"No," Charlie whispered.

"Want to go do something fun? See a movie? Get some ice cream?"

Charlie loved ice cream and movies, but she didn't feel like having fun today. She just wanted to sit in her room and feel sorry for herself. She was supposed to be on her way to gymnastics practice to get ready for the parade the next day. Instead, they went home.

*My dumb ol' broken leg ruined everything,* she thought.

# Chapter 5
# Picnic Party

Charlie laid on her bed with her leg propped up on some pillows. She tried to read a book but all the words kept jumbling together. She drew a picture of a dog-lion-flamingo then crumpled it in a ball and tossed it on the floor. She looked at the clock and sighed.

"I'm SO bored," she groaned. She'd hoped Leo would come over and play board games or watch TV or just something but he didn't even call. Her dad poked his head into her room and said "Dinner!" way too cheerfully.

"I'm not hungry," she said. She squeezed her eyes shut, then opened just one to see if her dad was still there. He wasn't.

He came back a minute later with a tray of food. Her mom came in with another tray. They put the trays down on her bed then plopped down on either side of her.

"Picnic in bed!" Her mom clapped her hands like this was the most exciting idea ever. Charlie giggled.

"That's my girl!" her dad said. He gave her a loud *mmm-wah* kiss on the top of her head. "I thought a grumpy troll had moved into your room!"

"Very funny, mister," Charlie said, wagging her finger at him. "I'm not a grumpy troll. I'm BROKEN!" She pointed to her cast. She wiggled her toes poking out from the end of it.

"It's not forever, squirt. You're gonna be just fine. Now eat this delicious feast of grilled cheese and broccoli before I eat it all." Her dad took a giant bite from his sandwich and made a loud noise.

"Chew with your mouth closed!" Charlie laughed. She took a bit of her sandwich, too. The gooey cheese tasted delicious, but the sadness in her belly made her not feel like eating.

"Can I call Leo?" she asked. "I want to know if the baby is here yet."

"I just talked to his mother, no baby yet," her mom said.

"Oh," Charlie said. "Well can I call him, anyway?"

"He's not home, honey," she said. "Come out to the living room, let's play a game!" She gathered up the trays and hurried out of Charlie's bedroom.

Charlie looked at her dad. He just shrugged his shoulders and made a silly face. "Let's go play a game in the living room. Your bed is full of crumbs now, you can't stay in here. It's dangerous."

She looked down at the bed. There were only a couple of crumbs. "You're a goofball," she said.

"Hop on," he said. She climbed on his back like she used to do when she was a little kid. He carried her out to the living room and placed her on the couch, then turned on the television.

"The weather for tomorrow's parade will be breezy and beautiful," the TV news weather guy said.

"Great," Charlie said. She stuck her tongue out at the TV. When the phone rang, she tried to jump up on her good leg but she lost her balance and fell back on the couch.

It was only one of her mom's friends, anyway. Not that mean ol' Leo, who wasn't even her friend anymore maybe.

# Chapter 6
# You Must Be Kidding

Charlie's mom woke her up before the sun was even awake.

"You need to shower, young lady. You haven't bathed since you broke your leg. You're going to start growing plants all over you, you're so dirty!"

Charlie grumbled into her pillow. Then she sat up straight, her eyes wide.

"That would be SO cool!" She imagined being covered in wildflowers and banana trees. She loved bananas. She flopped back down and covered her face with her pillow. "I don't have to shower now because I want to be covered in plants. Night, night!" she mumbled.

Her mom pried the pillow out of her hands and said "Up!" like she meant serious business. Charlie swung her legs to the side of the bed and grabbed her crutches. "Why so early?" she whined.

"We have things to do," her mom said. She followed her to the bathroom and put a white garbage bag over Charlie's cast, then tied it real tight around the top. Then, she put some tape around it so no water could get in.

"Do you need me to stay in case you need help?"

Charlie didn't want her mom to help her shower. She was too grown up for that! But she was also afraid that she might slip because of her dumb broken leg.

"Yes, please," Charlie said.

Showering was a tricky business. Charlie wobbled on her good leg as she tried not to put any weight on the broken one. She washed her hair as quickly as she could, then got out of there before she broke another leg.

"I'm not doing that again till this thing is off," she said, wrapping herself in a fluffy towel. Her mom laughed.

"Yeah, we'll see about that," she said. "Chariot! We need a chariot in here!"

Charlie's dad appeared in the doorway and scooped her up like a baby. It made her laugh. Her took her to her room and set her down on the bed. "I'm going to make breakfast," he said. "Toasted frog boogers and grapes!"

"Ew!" Charlie shook her head and laughed. Her mom laughed too. She helped Charlie get dressed in shorts and a sparkly top. Then she dried her hair with the hair dryer.

"Where are we going?" Charlie asked.

"Oh, nowhere special," her mom said. She hummed as she wove Charlie's hair into a French braid.

"Where is nowhere special?" Charlie pried.

"Just the grocery store and stuff."

Charlie groaned. "You're going to make me walk around the grocery store?" She pointed at her leg.

"Yup," her mom said.

# Chapter 7
# Liar , Liar

It turned out that Charlie's mom was a liar liar pants on fire. But it was a good lie, because surprise! The car did not stop at the grocery store! It didn't stop until they got downtown to the Blueberry Festival.

She only had to walk on her crutches a short distance to a special tent. It was full of wheelchairs for rent. She left her crutches with the woman in charge.

Charlie felt a little like a baby in a stroller. Her dad made car noises as he pushed through the crowd. She covered her eyes and giggled. When she uncovered her eyes, she saw Leo and his family standing next to her gymnastics coach. Leo waved his arms at her like a wild man. He had the biggest smile she'd ever seen.

She felt grumpy at him for a second. Then she felt curious. Everyone was staring at her kind of funny with giant grins.

Then, they moved apart and Leo said "Ta- Da!"

Charlie's mouth opened wide. She looked at the glittering float then back at Leo. "Is that for me?"

"Yep! I built it so you could still lead the parade!" Leo looked like he might bust open any second with all the excitement.

"WE built it." Leo's older brother Rommy grinned and rumpled Leo's hair.

Charlie couldn't believe it. She also said a quick sorry in her head for thinking grumpy thoughts about Leo. Because her very best bud in the whole world just saved her big break!

"Is that why you were ignoring me?" she asked.

Leo grinned and stuck his hands in his pockets. He looked shy for a minute. "I wasn't ignoring you, I was afraid I'd accidentally tell you the secret so I had to keep my lips zipped," he said. "And we were building like crazy!"

"I've never had so much fun with glitter," Leo's mom said. Her baby belly was so big, Charlie didn't know how she wasn't falling over.

"Is that baby going to stay in there forever, or what?" Charlie joked.

"I hope not!" Leo's mom laughed.

Leo's brothers wanted to sign Charlie's cast. So did Coach, and Leo's parents. They took turns drawing funny things. Then it was show time.

"Let's get you in here and over to the parade line up," Coach said.

She helped Charlie get up from the wheelchair. Her dad and Leo's dad lifted her onto the float. Leo told her they made it from wood scraps and bike tires and stuff. It was painted purple to match her cast and it sparkled with glitter and shiny plastic gems. It even had a special seat for her to sit in with a place to prop up her leg. A box full of beads sat next to her.

"Good luck, honey!" her mom blew her a kiss.

"Break a leg, squirt!" her dad joked. Everyone laughed. Charlie groaned.

Leo and Coach each grabbed a handle and pushed the float toward the others that were lined up for the parade. Charlie waved at everyone as they made their way to the front.

Charlie's gymnastics team was warming up at the start line. They cheered when they saw Charlie. Even Karrington!

"This float is magical!" Karrington squealed. She reached up and squeezed Charlie's hand. "Sorry about your leg."

"Um, thanks," Charlie said. *Today is full of surprises*, she thought to herself.

Charlie watched the team do back handsprings and cartwheels and stretches. Then a lady shouted into a megaphone. "It's go time, people!"

The team lined up in their positions. Leo and Coach pushed Charlie to the front. It was really happening. She was leading the parade!

"This makes you the parade's grand marshal, you know," Coach said.

"Thanks to my very best friend in the whole universe!" Charlie said. "Thank you, Leo. Thank you, Coach. This is the best day ever!"

When the music started, Charlie was ready with her arms loaded with strands of beads in every color. As they made their way through the streets, she waved and smiled and tossed beads toward the cheering crowd. She tried to make sure every kid got a strand. Her leg ached a little and her arms ached a lot from all the waving and tossing, but she didn't care.

She saw lots of her classmates and other kids she recognized from school. They screamed her name when they saw her. She'd never been so happy.

Charlie's parents were waiting at the end of the parade route. Their faces looked excited.

"You did great, squirt!" her dad said, helping her down from the float.

# Chapter 8
# Surprise!

"So proud of you, Charlie." Her mom kissed the top of her head. "Now, hop in your chariot, because we have to get out of here quick. You're coming with us Leo," she said.

"Wha – why? Is it – " Leo stammered.

"Your family is on the way to the hospital, kiddo. You're going to be a big brother!" Charlie's mom said.

Charlie squealed. Leo looked like he might faint. Charlie's dad laughed.

Charlie scooted over in her wheelchair, making room for Leo. "Hop in, big bro," she said. He squeezed in next to her.

"Ready, set, let's roll, tornadoes!" her dad said, and began pushing them through the crowd.

\*\*\*\*\*\*

Leo's brothers met them in the hospital waiting room. They said the baby would arrive any minute.

Just then, Leo's dad burst through the door. He was out of breath like he'd just run a race. He was also laughing so his words sounded all jumbled up.

"It's a, It's a ..." he started, then hunched over laughing like a madman. "It's a ..."

"It's a what?" everyone shouted at once.

Leo's dad took a deep breath. He looked around at everyone and his eyes looked wet with tears.

"It's a girl!" He threw out his arms and did a crazy little dance. Everyone gasped or squealed or laughed or said "No way!" Some people did all of those things.

"What's her name?" Charlie asked.

"Well, since we've been calling her Joe all this time, we're going to name her Joelle," Leo's dad said.

"Can I come over after school and hold her? I can babysit! I am very good at sitting these days," Charlie pointed to her cast.

Leo's dad gave her a high-five. "You're hired!"

Charlie wanted to run and jump and climb again, but sitting around holding a tiny baby all afternoon didn't sound like a bad way to spend the next six weeks while her leg healed.

"I'm hired!" Charlie laughed. "It's my big break!"

## Reflection

When I felt my leg go SNAP!, I was so
scared. It really hurt. The doctors made
it better, but it took a long time to heal.
The worst part was thinking my best bud
Leo didn't want to be my friend anymore
because I couldn't run and play. Missing
out on leading the parade stunk, too. But
Leo DID still want to be my best bud! And
the parade turned out better than I thought
it would. This bummer broken leg sure
made me see that being a great friend is
the best thing you can ever do for someone.
I hope no one ever breaks their parts, but
if they do, I'm going to be a super friend
to them!

## Discussion Questions

1. Why was Charlie so disappointed when the doctor gave her the news about her leg?

2. Why did Charlie think Leo didn't want to be her friend anymore?

3. Did Leo do anything wrong by sneaking around and avoiding Charlie?

4. Why was Leo's dad so surprised at the hospital?

5. Did Charlie make the best of the situation after she came home from the hospital? Why or why not?

## Vocabulary

Some of these words have more than one meaning. Do you know them all? Can you think of fun ways to use all of these words in a story?

ambulance
chariot
crutches
distraction
festival
float
fractured
paramedics
scraps

## Writing Prompt

Finish this sentence and write about your own experiences.
I remember a time when I was sick or hurt, and my friend helped me by ...

## Q & A with Author Reese Everett

### Have you ever broken a bone?
I HAVE broken a bone. Two, actually. My pinky toes on both feet were both broken at different times. Once, I stubbed my foot on a piece of furniture. The other time I ran right into the back of my son's shoe with my toe. Both times made me realize just how much we use our pinky toes when we walk. It hurts when they're broken!

### Have you ever felt like a friend was ignoring you?
I've had my share of misunderstandings with friends. I've learned along the way that it is best to ask questions and communicate. If you assume the worst, you may be worrying for no reason. Sometimes your friends are just busy. And sometimes they might be hiding a secret – and doing something nice just for you.

### Have you even performed in a parade?
I have been in several parades. When I was a young girl, I was a baton twirler. We wore sequined leotards and twirled our batons as we marched. It was a lot of fun!

## Connections

Do you have a friend who's sick or injured? Making a card or poster is a simple way to cheer them up and show you care. You also can make cards and crafts for kids you don't know who are sick in the hospital.

## Websites to Visit

www.hugsandhope.org

http://media.chop.edu/data/files/pdfs/ injury-prevention-kohls-injury-prevention-book.pdf

http://www.artistshelpingchildren.org/ paradescraftsideasdecorationskids.html

## About the Author

Reese Everett is a children's book author from Tampa, Florida. She loves her four kids, silly adventures, and sunny days at the beach. And avocadoes. Her favorite thing to see is people being kind and helpful to others.

## About the Illustrator

Sally Anne Garland
was born in Hereford
England and moved to
the Highlands of Scotland
at the age of three. She
studied Illustration at
Edinburgh College of Art
before moving to Glasgow where she now
lives with her partner and young son.